Honeypot Hill

Saffron Thimble's
Sewing Shop

To the City

The Orchards

Paddle Steamer
Quay

Aunt
Marigold
General
Store

Lavender Valley
Garden Centre

Healing House and Garden

The Worthingtons' House

Lavender Lake

Bumble Bee's Teashop

Lavender Lake
School of Dance

SCHOOL

Hedgerows Hotel
Where Mimosa lives

Peppermint
Pond

Rosehip School

Summer Meadow

Christmas Corner

Wildspice Woods

Honeysuckle Cottage
Poppy's House

Forget-Me-Not Cottage
Grandpa's House and Office

Poppy Field

N
W — E
S

Honeypot Cottage
Honey and Granny Bumble's House

Blossom
Bakehouse

Cornsilk Castle
and Courtyard

Village Hall

Sage's
Vet Surgery

Post Office

River Swan

Beehive
Beauty Salon

Barley Farm
The Meadowsweets' House

Riverside
Stables

Honeypot Hill
Railway Station

To Camomile Cove
via Periwinkle Lane

Join Princess Poppy on more adventures . . .

★ The Birthday ★

★ Ballet Shoes ★

★ Twinkletoes ★

★ The Fair Day Ball ★

★ The Play ★

THE WEDDING
A PICTURE CORGI BOOK 978 0 552 55339 1

First published in Great Britain by Picture Corgi,
an imprint of Random House Children's Books

This edition published 2006

3 5 7 9 10 8 6 4

Text copyright © Janey Louise Jones, 2006
Illustration copyright © Picture Corgi Books, 2006
Illustrations by Veronica Vasylenko
Design by Tracey Cunnell

The right of Janey Louise Jones to be identified as the author of this work has been
asserted in accordance with the Copyright, Designs and Patents Act 1988.

Picture Corgi Books are published by Random House Children's Books,
61–63 Uxbridge Road, London W5 5SA, a division of The Random House Group Ltd,
London, Sydney, Auckland, Johannesburg and agencies throughout the world.
THE RANDOM HOUSE GROUP Limited Reg. No. 954009
www.kidsatrandomhouse.co.uk
www.princesspoppy.com

A CIP catalogue record for this book is available from the British Library.

Printed in China

Princess Poppy

The Wedding

Written by Janey Louise Jones

PICTURE CORGI

With all my love to Matthew,
who makes all my dreams come true

★

The Wedding

featuring

Honey

★

Grandpa

★

Granny Bumble

★

Princess Poppy

Mum

★

David Sage

♥

Saffron Thimble

♥

Poppy and her best friend Honey were helping Granny Bumble decorate the great hall at Cornsilk Castle in preparation for cousin Saffron's wedding to David, the Honeypot Hill vet. Grandpa was there too, but was not being much help at all!

"I'm so excited," said Poppy.

"Me too," replied Honey. "We're so lucky to be flower girls."

"I know," replied Poppy as she skipped over to one of the huge windows and peeped out onto the driveway. "Oh, look, everything is arriving."

Flowers and balloons were brought in . . .

then came a three-tiered wedding cake
and fresh strawberry cupcakes.

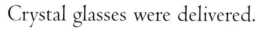

Crystal glasses were delivered.

And the violinist and the
photographer arrived.

Everyone in Honeypot Hill was busy trying to make Saffron and David's wedding the most perfect day ever.

But the final delivery was the most exciting of all . . .

A little van drew up outside the castle and beeped its horn.

"Mum's here with the dresses," said Poppy. "Let's go and help her. I can't wait to see them again!"

Poppy and Honey's dresses were gorgeous . . .

but Saffron's dress was truly perfect – just as she had pictured it!

TOP SECRET FILE ! <u>My Wedding Dress</u> by Saffron Thimble

head-dress
fresh flowers –

side

antique lace edging

front

satin ribbon

fresh gardenia

veil / tulle head-dress

back

short veil

choker with single pearl

hair loose

my bouquet

pink satin underskirt

small train

satin shoes

layer of oyster/rose chiffon

notes

will need..
(from Aunt Marigold's store)

10m chiffon
5 m tulle
satin ribbon
antique lace
underskirt

Take train to town for
Satin shoes
necklace
gifts for Poppy + Honey

flowers from the Lavender Garden

Something old ♥ something new ♥ something borrowed ♥ something blue

David

I love David

Grandpa helped Poppy and Honey carry the dresses upstairs to the little dressing room where Saffron, Poppy and Honey would get ready later that day.

"I'm going to see whether they need any help in the great hall," said Grandpa. "Make sure you hang those beautiful dresses up carefully."

"I can't wait till later," Poppy whispered to Honey, "I've just
got to try my dress on now!"

Honey agreed. They *had* to see how they looked. They shut
the door and carefully stepped into the gorgeous chiffon dresses.

Honey helped Poppy with
the pink rosebud buttons.

Poppy tied Honey's
green satin sash.

They did up each other's
pink silk neck chokers

and stepped into their
little pink slippers.

"Wow!" breathed Poppy. "These really are perfect princess dresses."

"They are perfect, but mine's definitely a fairy dress!" giggled Honey.

Then they held hands and danced around the dressing room.

"We'd better take them off now before someone sees us," said Honey, suddenly feeling worried.

They reluctantly took the dresses off and hung them back on their satin hangers. Then Poppy had a thought . . .

She looked at Honey. Then she looked at Saffron's wedding dress. Then she looked back at Honey.

"Poppy! You CANNOT try that one on," said Honey.
"It's Saffron's special dress."

 "I'm sure she wouldn't mind," said Poppy. "In fact, if she
were here, she would probably ask me if I wanted to try it on."

Poppy took the precious wedding dress off its hanger and stepped inside Saffron's magical silk gown. It was much too big for her.

"I may as well put Saffron's shoes on too — just to get the right look," explained Poppy.

"I'll look in the mirror and then I promise I will take it off," she said as she teetered across the dressing room, humming *Here Comes the Bride.*

But then . . .

Poppy lost her balance and fell over, catching the heel of Saffron's shoe in the hem of the dress.

Riiiiip! Poppy collapsed in a crumpled heap.

"Oh no!" she cried. "I've torn Saffron's dress. I've ruined it!"

"Hang it back up again," suggested Honey. "Maybe no one will notice."

Poppy quickly took the dress off and hung it up. But at the back of her mind she thought about how kind Saffron was and how upset she would be to find her wedding dress had been ruined. "Oh no," thought Poppy. "What should I do?"

The girls trudged downstairs and found Saffron in the great hall admiring the garlands of cornflowers, honeysuckle and jasmine that had been put up.

"Hi, girls! What do you think of the flowers?" asked Saffron.

Instead of answering her, both little girls burst into tears.

"Don't you like them?" asked Saffron, sounding surprised.

"It's not the flowers!" explained Poppy. "It's your dress!"

"You don't like my dress?"

"Yes. Yes, we do! It's just that, well, erm, you see, I tried it on and, erm, I've ruined it," sobbed Poppy.

Saffron was horrified, but she could see how upset and sorry Poppy was, so she tried hard not to show it.

"I had better go and have a look then. I'm sure it can't be that bad," said Saffron, sounding calmer than she felt.

Poppy and Honey followed Saffron to the dressing room,
dragging their feet all the way.

"What *were* you thinking, Poppy?" asked Saffron.

"I don't know," sobbed Poppy. "Your dress is so lovely, I
just wanted to wear it – just once! I am really, really sorry."

Saffron looked at the damage, then looked at the clock.

"Don't worry, Poppy," said Saffron kindly, "it's not too bad, but we have only got two hours, so you will have to help me fix this . . .

I need the pink sewing box from my shop and some more chiffon from Aunt Marigold's General Store. Why don't you go and ask Grandpa to help you fetch them?"

Saffron fixed the dress and they managed to get ready just in time!

Everyone gasped as the beautiful bride and her two little
flower girls walked into the chapel.

Poppy felt so happy, and relieved that everything had
turned out all right – the day *was* going to be perfect after all.

After the ceremony, Saffron gave Poppy
and Honey a pink satin handbag each,
to thank them for being such special
princess flower girls. Then everyone
partied into the night in the beautiful
great hall at Cornsilk Castle.

"Grandpa, am I still a real princess?" Poppy asked him as they danced around the great hall together.

Grandpa paused. "Yes, Poppy, when you're telling the truth you are. You'll always be my princess."